TALL TAILS

WINGIN' IT WITH THE WRIGHT BROTHERS

ENJOY ALL OF THE BOOKS IN THE
TALL TAILS SERIES:

TALL TAILS #1
Wingin' It with the Wright Brothers

COMING SOON:

TALL TAILS #2
Cross-Country with Lewis and Clark

TALL TAILS

Wingin' It with the WRIGHT BROTHERS

BY DONA SMITH

ILLUSTRATIONS BY
GUY FRANCIS

A
LITTLE APPLE
PAPERBACK

SCHOLASTIC INC.
New York Toronto London Auckland Sydney
Mexico City New Delhi Hong Kong Buenos Aires

ISBN 0-439-29742-7

Design by Joyce White

12 11 10 9 8 7 6 5 4 3 2 3 4 5 6 7 8/0

Printed in the U.S.A. 40

First printing, December 2003

For Billy

Dear Reader,

I have learned to believe the unbelievable. Read on, and you will, too.

It all started the day I brought my terrier puppy, Elvis, home. Elvis was different from any other dog I had known. For one thing, he loved to read. Strange as it sounds, I often found him curled up with a book.

Then one day Elvis wrote me a note. I wouldn't have believed it if I hadn't seen it with my own eyes. Here is what he wrote:

Dear Dona,

Please follow me to the park. It is time for you to know the truth.

Elvis

Of course I followed him. What else could I do? When we got to the park Elvis began to dig and dig. Soon he uncovered an old wooden trunk with a bone carved on the front. He nudged it open with his nose and gave me a long look.

Inside the trunk I found several dog-eared volumes. Each was a diary, telling about history from a dog's point of view. I read them and discovered that dogs created many of history's golden moments and great inventions. I showed the diaries to my editor, Joy Peskin. We decided that we must publish them. Now it is time for you, too, to know the truth.

Best Wishes,
Dona Smith
Joy Peskin
Elvis

Chapter 1
May 1899

May 8, 1899

My name is Angus, and I'm not a puppy anymore.

So I've given up chasing bicycles. I've quit chewing chairs and high-button shoes. I no longer tug at ladies' long skirts. I've stopped barking at horses and buggies.

I've stopped growing, too. Mostly, I'm happy with the way I turned out. I'm happy with my reddish coat. I'm happy with the whiskers around my nose, and I'm happy with my short tail. But I'm not happy with my size.

I'm one of the smallest dogs in Dayton, Ohio. I'm a full-grown Border terrier, and I'm only about a foot tall. That means there isn't much for me to see. Who wants to look at shoes all the time? Who wants to eyeball dust balls? Boring!

When I was a puppy, I used to jump on the furniture to change my view. Now I know better. The people who adopted me don't like when I do that.

I live in a house with Wilbur and Orville Wright and their sister, Katharine. They're all grown up, too, but they are older than I am. Wilbur is 32, Orville is 27, and Katharine is 24. I'm only two years old.

The other day I got to thinking. If I were taller, I could see more stuff. But I could see even more if I could fly. Instead of looking up at everything, I'd look down for a change. I could see the whole world. The idea got my tail wagging!

I tried to tell my best friend, Nibbles, how I felt. He is a house mouse. Nibbles and his family live in the walls. Mice *like* the view from the floor.

Nibbles didn't want to talk about flying. He

was afraid it would make him dizzy. So he gave me this diary and told me to write about it instead.

May 11, 1899

I had never heard of a diary. Nibbles had to explain what it was. He told me that a diary is a book of your own. You write about yourself and your dreams. You write about your family and your friends.

"I can't write any more than I can fly," I told him. Then he told me something that rolled me over. He said that dogs were born knowing how to write. His mother told him so.

I grabbed a pen in my teeth and gave it a try. Sure enough, it was as easy as chewing on a bone.

Then I asked if mice could write. He said no. In fact, dogs were the only animals he knew that could write for sure.

I'm glad dogs can write. I wish we could fly, too.

May 15, 1899

I've got a new hobby — bird-watching.

All day long I stare at the birds flying in the sky. I try to pretend I'm a bird, too. If I were a bird, I wouldn't have to look up at everything anymore. I could soar above the clouds and see the whole world.

I'm a bird. I'm a bird. I'm a bird. I say the words to myself again and again.

I tell myself I have wings and feathers. I tell myself that I don't bark, I tweet. I even tell myself that I like to eat worms.

So far, it hasn't worked. I tried eating worms. Ick! No thanks. I'd rather have a bone any day. Besides, I'd look funny with wings and feathers. What dog wouldn't?

I guess I don't want to be a bird. But I still want to fly like one. What freedom! What happiness!

May 16, 1899

Fifi, the hound from around the corner, says happiness is right under your own backyard. Burying bones is what she lives for.

Fifi thinks flying is for the birds. So does Chester, Katharine's know-it-all cat. When I told Fifi and Chester that I wanted to fly, they laughed at me.

"If you were supposed to fly, you would have been born with wings," Chester said, and licked his whiskers. "Do as I say and get your head out of the clouds."

Fifi shook her big droopy head. "Forget that doggone idea right now!" she ordered.

Sometimes Fifi and Chester are so bossy that it makes me angry. But I can't stay mad for long. The two of them have looked out for me since I was a pup.

I was born on a farm. When the Wright brothers brought me home, I was only 11 weeks old. I'll never forget that dark and stormy night!

I didn't want to leave my mom and dad. But my parents told me all puppies need homes of their own. Now I know they were right.

At first I was scared. Then Fifi showed me how to fetch. She taught me not to be afraid of other dogs. Chester wouldn't let the neighborhood cats pick on me. The two of them helped me grow up.

I know that Fifi and Chester are older and wiser than I am. I know I should listen to what they say. But I've just got to fly.

May 19, 1899

Today I was all set to go bird-watching. Then I saw Nibbles. He was sitting alone in a corner. He looked so sad that even his whiskers drooped.

"What's wrong?" I asked.

"You never play with me anymore," he said. "All you do is watch birds."

I realized it was true, and I felt bad about ignoring Nibbles. I said I was sorry. Then I told him I watched birds because flying had become my dream.

Nibbles shook his head. "If I were you, I wouldn't want one more thing," he said. "My dream is to be a pet. You don't know what it's like having to hide all day long. You don't know what it's like to have someone chase you with a broom."

Poor Nibbles. I don't know why people don't like mice. I never thought of how lucky I am to be a pet. And how lucky I am to live with the Wrights.

May 23, 1899

Wilbur, Orville, and Katharine are like best friends. They go on picnics and bike rides together. They go camping together. At home, they always eat supper together. After that, they sit around and talk. Last night I listened while I gnawed on my bone.

"People are too quick to make fun of new ideas," said Wilbur. I could have told him that people weren't the only ones.

"You're right," Katharine agreed. "Just look at my new sewing machine. It practically sews by itself. Why, some people still laugh when I tell them a machine can sew."

"I'll tell you something else," said Orville. "In a few years, boys won't have to go around lighting the streetlamps. Soon they will be lit with *electricity* instead of a flame. I've been reading about it."

"I think you're right," said Wilbur. "Soon there will be all sorts of new inventions."

Suddenly, a thought popped into my head. Why couldn't someone invent a flying machine for a dog? I looked at Wilbur and Orville and Katharine. Couldn't one of them figure it out? They were all smart, and they all liked new ideas.

I thought about it for a while. Katharine was usually busy teaching high school. Wilbur and Orville had the bike shop. That would be a good place to build the flying machine. They could use the tools they used to make bicycles.

I decided I'd have to let the Wright brothers

know I wanted to fly. But how? Sometimes they understood my barking, but lots of times they didn't.

I decided to write them a note. When they read it, they would understand. What a great idea!

Later

Dear Wilbur and Orville,

You guys are real pals. Have you noticed what a good dog I've been lately? I haven't chewed any shoes. I don't whine for scraps at the table. I don't jump on the furniture. Doesn't a good dog deserve a reward?

I really want to fly. If you would build me a flying machine, I would be very happy. I promise that I would never be a bad dog again.

Building a flying machine could be lots of fun. It would be a change from making bicycles, too.

Love,
Angus

P.S. I would let you ride in it sometimes.

May 24, 1899

Writing a note wasn't such a great idea after all. I found that out last night.

I was lying on the porch. My diary was in front of me and I had a pen in my teeth. I had just finished my note and I was reading it over. I thought it looked pretty good. I was ready to tear the note out of the diary when Fifi and Chester showed up. That is when things went wrong.

"Grrr!" Fifi shoved my diary under a chair. "What do you think you're doing? Somebody might see you!"

"So what?" I asked.

Fifi and Chester looked at each other. Then they both went bananas. Chester let out a yowl. Fifi looked angry enough to bite me.

"People aren't supposed to know dogs can write," she said. "They aren't ready for it. They think they are the only creatures smart enough to do that."

"You know what happens to animals who

act too smart for their own good?" Chester asked. "They wind up in a three-ring circus. You'll get stuck between the sword swallower and the bearded lady."

I scrambled to my paws and tucked my tail between my legs. That sounded scary. I didn't want to be taken away from my home. I didn't want strangers to stare at me.

"That is why I never told you that dogs could write," said Fifi. "Writing only causes trouble."

Fifi looked me in the eye. "Take an old dog's advice," she said. "Don't learn too many new tricks. Stick to *woof, ruff-ruff,* and *yip.* And never let a human know you can write. When you're older, you'll understand."

I'd heard that last line before. My mother used to say it a lot.

When Fifi and Chester were gone, Nibbles appeared. He had been hiding, but he heard the whole thing.

"I'm sorry, Angus," he said. "I didn't know

your writing had to be a secret. I never thought it could get you in big trouble."

I guess Nibbles and I have a lot to learn.

May 29, 1899

I almost decided to forget about my dream. Then I remembered what my father and mother used to say: "A terrier never gives up."

I've made up my mind to fly, and I'm not going to give up.

Chapter 2
June 1899

June 8, 1899

I came up with a plan. Every time Wilbur or Orville watched *me,* I would watch birds. That's how I would let the Wright brothers know I wanted to fly.

Well, I've been at it for a week. So far, the Wright brothers don't get the point. They just chuckle about how much I like birds.

Orville has started calling me "bird dog." Almost every day he tells me a bird joke. Here's one:

What do you call a box full of ducks? *A box of quackers.*

He kept saying it again and again, but I got it the first time. Quackers, like crackers.

Yesterday he called me a birdbrain. I knew he was only kidding, but my tail wasn't wagging. Wilbur didn't think it was funny, either. He said, "That's enough, Orv."

Then Orville patted me on the head and said he was sorry. He always listens to Wilbur.

June 12, 1899

Nibbles asked if my plan was working. I had to tell the truth. I couldn't get through to the Wright brothers. I didn't know how to get them to build me a flying machine. I asked Nibbles if he had any ideas.

"Just get one brother to notice how much you want to fly," he said. "Get one in your corner and you've got them both. The two of them think alike. They can practically read each other's minds."

Before Nibbles could say any more, Katharine came through the door. Nibbles had to run and hide. Poor Nibbles, always having to run away.

June 13, 1899

Nibbles is a real smart mouse. What he told me about the Wright brothers yesterday was true. Last night after supper I watched them like a watchdog. I listened and learned, too.

"Hey, Orv," Wilbur said. "Would you hand me the . . ."

"Newspaper?" Orville smiled and passed it to him. How did he know what Wilbur wanted?

Then Orville said, "Wilbur, where did I put those . . . ?"

Wilbur didn't even look up from the newspaper. "The scissors? You put them in a desk drawer," he answered.

The Wright brothers finished each other's sentences all the time! It *was* like they could read each other's minds.

I guess I was so used to being around them I hadn't really noticed. But Nibbles had.

June 14, 1899

Now I know that Nibbles was right. All I have to do is get one Wright brother to realize that I want to fly. Which brother should I choose?

First I thought about Orville. He talks a lot. He is always laughing and making jokes.

Next I thought about Wilbur. He is quieter. It might be easier to get his attention. Then I remembered how Orville always listens to Wilbur.

My mind is made up. I'll go to work on Wilbur. I'll show him how much I want to fly. Then he'll get Orville to help build me a flying machine.

June 15, 1899

I've started following Wilbur around. I follow him when he goes for a walk. I follow him to the store. I follow him to the bicycle shop.

When I see a bee, I bark. When I see a fly, I bark.

Chester follows us both around. He knows what I'm trying to do, and he says I'm wasting my time. "Wilbur won't think about building you a flying machine. He'll think you're a bad dog. That barking will get you in trouble."

I'll show that know-it-all cat a thing or two.

June 18, 1899

I hate to admit it, but Chester was right. Yesterday I was following Wilbur around, barking at birds. All of a sudden, he looked down at me and scowled.

"Stop that barking, Angus! Bad dog!" he said. "Get back in the house!"

I walked back with my tail between my legs. Naturally, Chester saw the whole thing.

"I told you so." He grinned.

All I could do was glare at him.

"What's the matter?" he asked with a smirk. "Cat got your tongue?"

Oh, that cat!

Later

Tonight, Wilbur told Katharine I'd been barking a lot. I thought she would be angry, but she wasn't. "Pay attention," she said. "Maybe he's trying to tell you something."

Katharine was always really good at understanding me. I walked over to her and wagged my tail. She reached down and patted me on the head. I couldn't resist giving Chester a smug look.

June 21, 1899

I think Katharine's words did the trick. Today, Wilbur and Orville went out to a field. I followed them.

When they got to the field, Wilbur stretched out on the grass. Pretty soon Orville did, too. I sat down beside Wilbur and stared up at the birds in the sky.

Soon I got so excited I couldn't sit still. I began to jump and bark. I waved my paws in the air. How I wished they were wings!

Orville paid no attention. He was jabbering away.

"Wait a minute," said Wilbur. "Look at Angus."

Orville looked at me and laughed. "Angus is bird-watching again."

"That dog wants to fly," said Wilbur. "I've been watching him. He's got me wanting to fly, too."

Wilbur was getting the idea! I leaped into the air and yelped.

"I guess you're right," Orville said. He looked up into the sky. "It would be a thrill, wouldn't it, Wilbur?"

"It sure would," Wilbur answered. Then he scratched my ears and said, "Wouldn't it, Angus?"

I wagged my tail and jumped in the air again.

At last, the Wright brothers know I want to fly. When will they start building my flying machine?

June 23, 1899

Something important happened today. The Wright brothers always come home for lunch in the same order. Wilbur is first. He does the same things every day. He puts his hat on a hook by the door. Then he combs his hair and washes his hands. He has a cracker and then he eats lunch.

When Orville comes in, he throws his hat anywhere. I don't know how he finds it later, but he always does. Wilbur is the one who forgets his hat after lunch, even though it's right there on the hook. He walks out the door without it all the time. Then he comes back for it a few minutes later.

I think Wilbur is forgetful because he daydreams. I do it, too. I daydream about flying all the time.

When I'm not thinking about flying, I'm thinking about eating. One good thing about living with the Wright brothers and their sister is the food. They are all good cooks, and they aren't stingy with the tidbits.

I'm under the table at every meal. I like to listen to the three of them talk. Sometimes when my mind is on meat loaf, words go in one ear and out the other. But not today.

"You were right about Angus," Wilbur told Katharine. "He was trying to tell me something. That dog wants to fly."

"Do you think it would be possible to build a flying machine, Katharine?" asked Orville. "Wilbur and I were thinking about it."

"Why not?" she answered. "I think it's a wonderful idea. If anyone can do it, the Wright brothers can."

"I'm glad you think so," said Wilbur. "We are planning to build a flying machine that will glide on the air. A glider."

"We'll have to learn about flying first," said Wilbur. "Then we'll start building."

Well, I was so happy I rolled over. Soon I will get off the ground. I, Angus, will be the first flying dog!

June 24, 1899

I told my friends about the flying machine. They didn't exactly jump for joy. Chester thought it was just a crazy idea. Nibbles said so, too. Then he winked at me.

He always pretends to agree with Chester. Who can blame a mouse for trying to stay on a cat's good side?

Fifi didn't say anything at first. She just scratched her ear with her back paw. She was having trouble with fleas.

When she spoke up, she told me to face facts. The flying machine probably wouldn't get off the ground. And I should forget about it, anyway. Because the Wright brothers were people. And I was a dog. So they'd never let me get near their flying machine.

I told her that she was wrong. The whole thing was my idea. They were building it for *me.*

She asked me if I'd heard them say so. I had to admit that I hadn't. But it didn't matter. I knew Wilbur and Orville. They wouldn't let me down.

June 25, 1899

I tried not to let what Fifi said get my tail dragging. The Wright brothers would get their flying machine off the ground. I had no doubt about it. They are like terriers. When they put their minds to something, they don't give up.

But Fifi's words had other doubts nipping at my heels. What if the flying machine wasn't for me? What if they were building it just for themselves?

I told myself it didn't matter. I would help the Wright brothers build their glider. Then they would let me fly it, too.

So starting right now, I'm going to learn all about flying. I'll try to figure out why birds can fly. I'll watch how the Wright brothers build their machine. And I'll write about it in this diary.

I'll write down everything that happens until the big day when I take to the air. My diary will become a history book about a dog's first flight!

June 26, 1899

I should never have told Chester my plan. He said that dogs don't write books, they chew them. That started an argument. Here's how it went:

"Dogs *do* write books!"

"Doggy don't!"

"Doggy do! Doggy do! Doggy doo-doo!"

Too late, I realized I'd been tricked.

"Doggy doo-*doo not* write books." Chester grinned. "Sneak into the library and see for yourself. Don't step in anything!"

Ha-ha. I'm going to wipe the smirk off that cat's face.

June 27, 1899

Chester gave me an idea. Last night I snuck into the town library. I was going to find some books written by dogs.

Otis Smoot, the night watchman, was asleep

on the job. His snoring made more noise than a barnyard at sunrise.

I snuck right past him and looked at all the shelves of books. There were so many. How could I tell which books were written by dogs?

Then I found a history book by someone named D. Oberman. *Doberman!* I figured the author was probably a dog, so I nosed the book off the shelf. It was called *Important Stuff in History.*

I began sniffing my way through the book. What I smelled wasn't good. There was no important stuff about dogs.

There was a section about inventors. They had names like Edison, Franklin, and Bell, not Trixie, Fido, and Rover.

There was a section about presidents, too. I didn't see any dogs' names there, either. In fact, there wasn't a single word about dogs in D. Oberman's whole book.

I didn't believe a dog would write a book with no dogs in it. So D. Oberman must not be a dog.

I backed down the aisle, looking at book after book. I just didn't know how to find one written by a dog.

Suddenly, I backed into a chair. *Crash!* It fell over.

Otis let out a noise like a pot boiling over. Then he whistled like a teakettle. Then he woke up.

I hightailed it out of the library as poor old Otis huffed and puffed after me. I'd better not go back.

June 29, 1899

I'm sure dogs have written plenty of books. I just haven't found them yet. That is why I'm staying away from Chester. He loves to say, "I told you so."

Today I caught him prowling around after me. Just then, the Wright brothers rode by on their bicycles. I ran after them and let Chester eat my dust.

I raced ahead, out toward a field. With a few *woof-woofs,* I signaled for the Wright brothers to follow. They did. It was as good a time as any to learn more about flying.

When we got to the field, we sat down and watched the buzzards fly. I watched carefully, and I noticed something. Their wings were curved, and the buzzards kept twisting them as they flew. When they turned, they lifted the front edge of one wing up. They folded the front edge of the other wing down. Why?

I thought of the paper gliders kids in our neighborhood made. Their wings were flat, and they didn't twist. They didn't stay up in the air very long, either. They teetered in the air and lost their balance.

It started me thinking. When I was a puppy, I couldn't stand up for very long at first. I had to learn to keep my balance. People had to learn to keep their balance to ride a bicycle, too.

I looked up at the birds again. The wheels in my mind started spinning.

Suddenly, I got it. The birds were twisting their wings to balance in the air! That was how they stayed up in the sky. The Wright brothers had to make the wings of their flying machine do the same thing.

June 30, 1899

Now what? I can't make my own flying machine. I may be able to write, but when it comes to building, I'm all paws. If I can't show the Wright brothers how to keep their machine in the air, I'll never get off the ground.

Nibbles told me not to worry. He said he knew I'd find a way. It's great to have a friend like Nibbles. But I'm not so sure he's right.

Chapter 3
July–August 1899

July 2, 1899

Yesterday I went down to the Wright's bicycle shop. I like the way it always smells of sawdust and oil and glue.

Making bicycles is messy work. Sometimes Wilbur gets his clothes covered with grease and grime. It doesn't bother him.

Orville doesn't like to get his clothes dirty. He always wears a blue-and-white apron to keep his pants and shirt spotless.

It's fun to watch the Wright brothers work on bicycles. I'd rather watch them work on the flying machine, though. I hope they start soon.

I guess the glider will look like a big bird. Will it be covered with feathers?

If the wings don't twist like a bird's, it won't stay in the air. I still haven't figured out how to tell them about it.

Later

It turns out that I was in for a big surprise. Today at the bike shop I heard the Wright brothers talking about the way birds fly. They know how birds twist their wings to balance in the air. They figured it out all by themselves!

Wilbur and Orville call the twisting *wing-warping.* They want to find a way to make their flying machine do the same thing.

July 4, 1899

Today was a holiday. Wilbur and Orville didn't go to the bicycle shop. Instead the Wright brothers and Katharine went on a picnic. When it got dark, they went to the park to watch fireworks. Katharine took Chester with them in a box.

Chester loves fireworks. They scare me. I don't like the smell or the noise.

Nibbles and I had the house to ourselves. We had so much fun. We played hide-and-seek. First I looked for Nibbles. Then Nibbles looked for me. That mouse is so good at hiding, I never found him once!

Now I'm tired. I hope the Wright brothers will start making the glider tomorrow.

July 6, 1899

"How is work going on the glider?" Nibbles asked me today. "Are the Wright brothers building it yet?"

"They keep talking about it," I told him. "But all they do is sit around drawing strange pictures. I don't know what they are. They don't look like birds."

Nibbles asked me to take him down to the bike shop. He wanted to see the pictures for himself.

When Wilbur and Orville came home for lunch, Nibbles and I sneaked out of the house.

The Wright brothers wouldn't like to see a mouse in their shop. We had to be careful that nobody spotted Nibbles along the way.

Nibbles helped me learn a lot that day. He scampered over the drawings in the shop's workroom. He took a good look at the pictures. Then he was quiet for a while, thinking things over.

"I think these drawings are sketches of glider parts," he said. "It's a good idea to draw pictures before you make something. You can figure out how to do it on paper."

He was one clever mouse. But he still had to hide when the Wright brothers came through the door. Wilbur almost saw him. Now Nibbles is afraid to go to the shop again. It sure must be tough to be a mouse.

July 11, 1899

I keep going to the bike shop every day. The Wright brothers still haven't begun building the glider. They have run into a problem. They can't figure out how to make the wings twist.

The man-made wings of their glider will be stiffer than a bird's wings. How can two stiff wings twist and balance the flying machine?

Wilbur and Orville tossed around ideas all day. They didn't come up with anything. I can't, either, and I've been racking my brain.

July 13, 1899

The Wright brothers still haven't figured out how to make the glider's wings twist. Neither have I.

I'm worried. "Just keep thinking," Nibbles told me. "You'll come up with an idea."

I wanted Nibbles to come back to the shop so he could look at the drawings again. He is so smart. I thought he might think of a way to make the wings of the glider bend.

Nibbles wouldn't come to the bike shop, though. He was too afraid of getting caught.

Later

I came home from the bike shop with my tail dragging. There still had been no progress.

Fifi tried to cheer me up. “Come on, kid,” she said. “Forget about flying and dig a few holes. You’ll feel better.”

“Come on, Angus. Buck up!” Nibbles told me. He couldn’t cheer me up, either. At least Chester didn’t give me a hard time. I think he was sorry to see me so sad.

July 14, 1899

I was so down in the dumps I didn’t even want to go to the bike shop today. But I did go, and I’m glad. I think I’ve found a way for the Wright brothers to solve their problem.

Wilbur and Orville spent the day cleaning up the shop. They threw out a lot of things. They tossed out old rags, pieces of wood, cans, and cardboard boxes.

After a while, there was a whole pile of trash. Wilbur threw a piece of cardboard on top. It was shaped like a long, thin rectangle. Something about it caught my eye.

Just then, Wilbur and Orville decided they

had done enough for one day. The two of them closed up the shop.

On the way home, I started thinking. The cardboard was stiff, but a long, thin piece could be twisted without breaking. Maybe the Wright brothers could make both wings of the glider out of a single long piece. Of course, they won't build their flying machine out of cardboard, but that piece in the trash pile could give them an idea. I can't wait for a chance to show it to them.

July 17, 1899

Today is Monday. The Wright brothers didn't go to the shop all weekend. This morning, Orville made some repairs around the house. Wilbur went to the shop by himself. I followed.

As soon as we got inside, I raced over and grabbed the long, thin piece of cardboard in my teeth. I held it down on the floor with my paw in the middle. Then I had to think.

I remembered what the birds did when they balanced in the air. They twisted the front edge of one wing up. They twisted the front edge of the other wing down.

I looked down at the cardboard. Then I pawed the front edge of one end up. I nosed the front edge of the other end down.

I took the cardboard over to where Wilbur was working. I put it in front of him and barked.

At first, he thought I wanted to play. He laughed and said he was too busy. I barked some more. He told me to be quiet a few times. Then he realized I was trying to tell him something.

Wilbur looked down at the piece of cardboard. Then he picked it up and turned it over in his hands. He twisted it the way I had.

"One end twists up and one twists down," he mumbled. "The piece of cardboard is stiff, but it's long and that makes it flexible. I've got it! We'll make both glider wings out of a single long piece. Then we can get the right twist."

Wilbur looked at me and scratched his head. "You helped me get an important idea," he said. "If only you understood what you just did."

I understood, all right. I had solved the wing-warping problem. Wilbur thought he had figured it out, but I don't care. At least he said I had helped.

I hope he'll thank me for helping by letting me fly in the glider. I just hope the Wright brothers start building it soon.

July 18, 1899

I was so excited! I couldn't wait to tell my friends what had happened with Wilbur and the wing-warping. Fifi and Chester hardly paid attention. I guess it was because they didn't believe the flying machine would work.

"Humans do the strangest things sometimes," said Fifi. "If Wilbur wants to play with cardboard, leave him alone. A grown-up dog has better things to do. Flying is for the birds!"

"You'd better mind your own business,"

Chester told me. "If you keep hounding the Wright brothers about that flying machine, you'll end up in the doghouse."

Only Nibbles was interested in my news. "Good for you, Angus!" he said.

July 24, 1899

I've been spending every evening at the Wright brothers' shop. When they are finished working on bicycles, they work on the glider.

I help out whenever I can. Sometimes I fetch a tool or a piece of wood. I can't wait until the glider is finished.

As the work goes on, I am getting more and more excited. The glider is small. It looks like it will be just my size. I don't want to get my hopes up, but I'm keeping my paws crossed. Maybe the Wright brothers are building the flying machine for me after all.

July 27, 1899

The glider is finished. Part of my dream has come true! The glider is much too small to hold one of the Wright brothers. They must have built the flying machine for me!

I can't wait to get off the ground. Will the glider fly like a bird?

July 28, 1899

When I told Nibbles about the glider, he was so happy that he ran in circles. Since he was afraid to go to the Wright brothers' bike shop and see it, I told him how it looked.

The flying machine has a five-foot wingspan. That means it is five feet from one wingtip to the other. Unlike a bird, it has *two* sets of wings. One is on the top, and one is on thc bottom.

The glider doesn't have any feathers. I guess it doesn't have to look *exactly* like a bird. It just has to do what a bird can do. Will it fly? When will I find out?

Chester heard me talking to Nibbles. "I'm giving you one more warning for your own good," Chester said. "Stay away from that flying machine."

August 7, 1899

The day to try out the flying machine finally came last week. When I got up that morning, I just knew it was time. My heart was doing flip-flops as I followed Wilbur and Orville to the shop. Katharine came along, too.

They all took the glider out to a field. Some boys from the neighborhood saw the flying machine and followed.

By the time we got to the field, I was worried. What if the flying machine didn't get off the ground? I didn't think I could stand it if the glider didn't fly.

I must have looked as worried as I felt. One of the boys pointed and said, "Look! That dog is frowning."

Then Wilbur sent the glider soaring into the sky. When I saw it fly, my frown turned upside down. It balanced in the air, just like a bird.

I figured Wilbur was getting the glider

warmed up for me. He flew it like a kite. Cords ran from the wingtips to sticks in his hands. When he tilted the sticks, the glider twisted its wings just like the buzzards did. The wing-warping worked perfectly.

The boys cheered. *Whoosh!* The flying machine soared and dipped and whirled. *Swoosh!* It swooped so low they had to duck.

That glider sure could fly. I couldn't wait any longer. I gave a mighty leap and jumped aboard.

Crash! I ended up in a tangle of string, wood, and bamboo. The boys all laughed, but Wilbur didn't. He looked at me and said the words I hate to hear. "Bad dog."

I've been in the doghouse ever since. Chester just had to say, "I told you so."

August 18, 1899

I didn't stay in the doghouse for too long. While I was there, I overheard the Wright brothers talking about the glider. I learned that

I didn't ruin the flying machine after all. What I broke was only a kite. It was a model for the real thing.

Wilbur and Orville wanted to see how a small glider worked before they built a bigger one. Are the Wright brothers smart or what?

I told Fifi about it. She said the Wright brothers were smart, all right. Smart enough not to let me near their flying machine the next time.

August 21, 1899

I'm still out of the doghouse, but I just heard some bad news. The Wright brothers told Katharine they are very busy making bicycles. They have to get lots of them ready to sell next spring and summer. Then they'll be busy selling bicycles and fixing bicycles. They won't have time to build the real glider for many months.

I'm going to put the diary away for a while. If I can't write about the flying machine, I'm not going to write at all.

Chapter 4
August 1900

August 1, 1900

Almost a whole year has passed since I last wrote! The Wright brothers didn't say a word about the glider for months. It had me worried. I was beginning to think they'd forgotten about it. Then, this summer, they began talking about flying again. I was so happy! They talked about wind a lot, too.

Wilbur said they couldn't fly the glider in Dayton, Ohio. It wasn't windy enough, and there wasn't enough space. He did some research and found the windiest places in the country. Then he wrote letters to people who lived in those places. I think he's trying to find the best place to fly.

August 6, 1900

The Wright brothers have been making drawings of glider parts again. This time the drawings are big. I think this glider will be bigger than any bird I have ever seen!

August 10, 1900

I found a letter when I was sniffing around in Wilbur's room. It was from a man named William Tate. He said he was the postmaster in Doggy Hawk, North Carolina. A man from the weather bureau there had told him about the Wright brothers.

Mr. Tate said Doggy Hawk was the perfect place to test the glider. There was lots of sand and lots of wind. The sand would make a nice, soft landing place.

Doggy Hawk. It must be a wonderful place for dogs. Even if it has a funny name.

You'd think there would be lots of dogwood trees in a place like Doggy Hawk. But the letter said there were hardly any trees at all. Only sand and wind. That made it a good place to fly.

August 12, 1900

Wilbur and Orville told Katharine they had decided to go to Doggy Hawk to test their glider. She wanted to hear all about the place. I figured my friends would, too. I got them all together to tell them the news. I also told them about the letter from William Tate.

"I saw the letter, too," said Chester. "It wasn't from Doggy Hawk. It was from Kitty Hawk."

"Uh-oh," said Nibbles. "Here we go."

"Doggy Hawk." I snarled.

"Kitty Hawk," hissed Chester.

"Doggy."

"Kitty."

Katharine told us to hush.

I know what I know. I saw what I saw. The place was called Doggy Hawk.

I've never been on a trip before. No matter what, I'm going on this one.

August 14, 1900

The Wright brothers have started building their glider. But I am not happy.

This afternoon I went to the bicycle shop. The minute I got there, I knew something was going on. Wilbur and Orville were cutting big pieces of wood. I heard them say it was ash wood, and that it was for the wings.

As soon as I heard the word *wings,* I got all excited. I started to jump and bark. I wanted to help.

That is when something terrible happened. Wilbur chased me out of the bike shop! "You can't come in while we are working on the glider!" he said.

I guess Wilbur still remembers that I ruined the little kite last year. It isn't fair. Flying was my idea in the first place. If not for me, the Wright brothers wouldn't even be making a glider. Now they won't let me near it.

August 15, 1900

"I told you the Wright brothers wouldn't let you near their flying machine," Fifi said when I told her what happened. "Forget all about it. A big thing like that will never get off the ground. That little glider they flew last year was only a kite."

I know Fifi is wrong. I can't stand to hang around the house while the Wright brothers build the glider. I've got to find a way to make them let me help.

August 16, 1900

Today I sat by the door of the bicycle shop all day. Every time I tried to go inside, one of the Wright brothers chased me out. I could hear them talking about the work they were doing. Wilbur is using steam to bend the pieces of ash wood. That is how he will make the wings curved.

August 17, 1900

Today I sat by the bicycle shop door again. It was just like yesterday. When I tried to go inside, the Wright brothers chased me out. I heard Orville say they would need to use lots of metal parts and steel wire to build the glider.

It's so hard to just sit by the door. I want to see what's going on! I want to bark, but I don't. I'm hoping that when Orville and Wilbur see what a good dog I can be, they'll let me inside.

August 20, 1900

Today I went to the bicycle shop and sat by the door *again.* After a while, Wilbur and Orville came out and looked at me.

"Angus has been behaving himself," said Wilbur.

"He has," Orville agreed. "He sure is interested in our glider. Should we let him come in and watch us build it?"

Wilbur thought it over for a minute. Then he said it was all right, but only if I was *very, very* good.

I was so happy that I wanted to bark, but I didn't make a sound. I just wagged my tail.

August 22, 1900

At first, the Wright brothers only let me watch them work. But I kept being very good. I didn't bark once. I didn't touch anything, either. Now they let me help, which makes me happy. They are cutting up lots and lots of wood. All day long I trot back and forth, carrying the pieces in my mouth and dropping them into piles.

While we worked today, I started wondering something. Which Wright brother was most like me?

Orville was always neat and tidy. That wasn't like me.

Wilbur wasn't so fussy. He doesn't care if his pants get wrinkled.

Katharine doesn't like it when Wilbur goes

around in wrinkled clothes. It's never long until she says something to him about it. Then Wilbur heats up the iron on the stove. He gives his pants a good pressing.

If I wore pants, I wouldn't care if they got wrinkled. I wouldn't press them, even if Katharine frowned. Ironing all four pant legs would be too much work.

Except for the neat and tidy part, Orville looks the most like me. That's because his big red mustache is almost the same color as my fur.

Orville talks all the time. He loves to play. Wilbur likes to daydream.

I guess they're *both* like me.

I was thinking of how well the brothers got along. Then, just like that, they started to fight. They never did that until they started to work on this glider.

August 29, 1900

Bicker, bicker, bicker. Wilbur and Orville were at it all day today. They argued about the best way to finish building the glider.

If one said something was wrong, the other said it was right.

If one said no, the other said yes.

When one said ’tis, the other said ’tisn’t.

They went on and on. “’Tis. ’Tisn’t. ’Tis. ’Tisn’t.”

Katharine told them to stop bickering. They acted like they didn’t even hear her.

August 30, 1900

The Wright brothers brought home a bunch of shiny white cloth. Orville got down on the floor and cut it into pieces. Wilbur sat at the sewing machine and stitched.

Chester watched Wilbur’s feet pumping the foot pedals.

The Wright brothers were making the cover for the glider’s wings.

So far, so good. I hoped they wouldn’t start bickering. But soon they were at it again. Naturally, it was something to do with the glider. This time they argued about how long to make the wings.

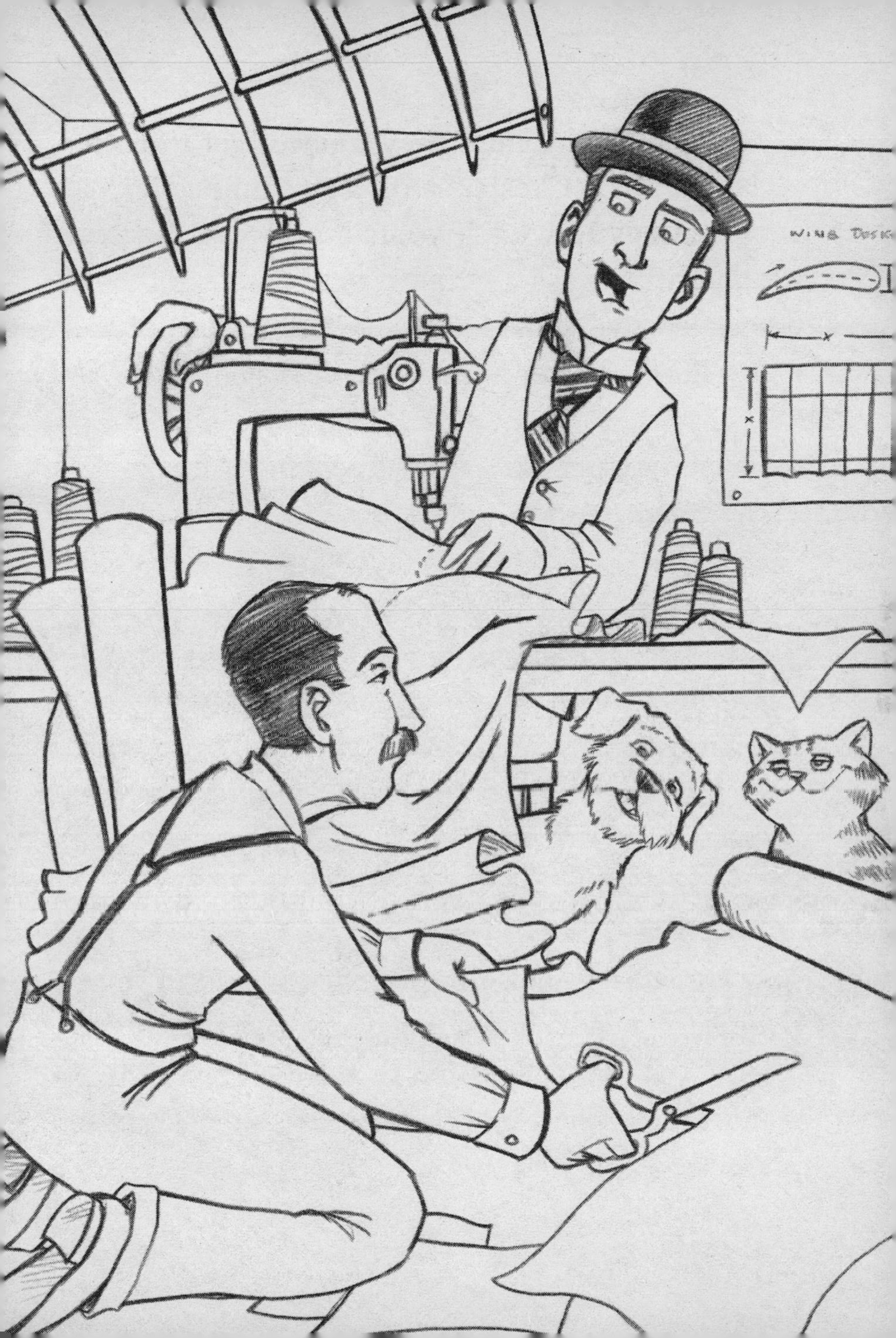
WING

"If this keeps up, they'll never get to Kitty Hawk," said Chester, with a sly smile.

"Doggy Hawk," I woofed.

"Kitty."

"Doggy."

Then Chester and I were at it again, too.

CHAPTER 5
September 1900

September 3, 1900

Today I went to the bike shop to keep an eye on Orville and Wilbur. As soon as I trotted in the door, I smelled trouble.

They were arguing again. They still couldn't agree on how long to make the wings. Wilbur said Orville was wrong. Then Orville said Wilbur was wrong. Orville walked away.

When Orville came back, Wilbur walked away. Then Wilbur came back. Orville said Wilbur was right after all. Then Wilbur said no, Orville was right. But Orville disagreed.

I tried to get them to play a nice game of fetch. It always calms me down. But they just kept bickering.

Then suddenly, they stopped and shook hands. They started working on the glider again, smiling and nodding.

"Now we've figured out the best way to build the glider," Orville said.

"That's right," said Wilbur. "We figured it out together."

Even when the Wright brothers bicker, they figure things out in the end. Too bad it doesn't work that way for Chester and me.

September 4, 1900

Most of the glider pieces are all finished. I heard the Wright brothers say they will put the flying machine together when they get to Doggy Hawk. If they put it together here, it would be too big to travel with.

I can't wait to see it all finished! The trip will be any day now.

Wilbur will go first. Orville will keep working at the bike shop for a while. Then he will follow.

I have a plan. When no one is looking, I'll

jump into Wilbur's canvas shoulder bag. He'll never know I'm there until we get to Doggy Hawk.

If I'm already there, he'll have to let me fly. Wilbur and I are pals.

September 5, 1900

Tomorrow is the big day.

The glider parts are packed up and ready to go. I'm packed, too.

I wonder how we will get to Doggy Hawk. Where will we sleep? What will we eat? Whatever is served, I will clean my plate like Mom taught me.

Nibbles promised to say good-bye to Chester and Fifi for me. If I told them about my plan, they'd try to talk me out of it.

"Are you scared?" Nibbles asked me tonight.

"Not one little bit," I told him. But maybe I am just a little bit scared.

September 6, 1900

So far my plan is working. I stowed away in Wilbur's shoulder bag. He never suspected a thing.

I heard Wilbur talking about going to the train station to catch a train. *What is a train?* I wondered. *Why do we have to catch it? Does it try to run away?*

When we got to the train station, I felt brave and peeked my head out of the bag. I took one look at the train and tucked my tail between my legs. I thought it was a huge, fire-breathing monster, and Wilbur was going to ride to Doggy Hawk on its back.

Now that we're inside, I can see that the train is not a monster. It's just a machine. I don't know why Wilbur said he had to catch it. All we had to do was get on.

Right after the train started moving, Wilbur fell asleep. I crawled out of the bag and hid under his seat.

The train may not be a monster, but it

sounds like one. The loud noise it makes is terrible. Plus, it rattles and shakes. Nibbles would get very dizzy.

Later

We'd been moving for a while, and Wilbur was still asleep. I was thinking about my best friend back home. Then guess who poked his head out of Wilbur's jacket pocket? Nibbles!

"Angus, I've got to toss my cookies," he said.

A woman saw him and screamed, "Eek!" Nibbles ran away.

Everybody started screaming and hopping around. It was like they'd been stung by a bunch of bees. Some people jumped up on their seats.

I got so excited, I started barking. I knew it would blow my cover, but I couldn't help myself.

Wilbur woke up then. When he saw me, his mouth dropped open. I was sure he would be angry. Instead, he laughed.

"Doggone it, Angus, you really love the flying machine, don't you?"

I barked and wagged my tail.

"You're a funny dog," he said.

After a long time, things were quiet again. Thank goodness Nibbles got away. I wonder where he is.

September 8, 1900

The train trip seemed to take forever. When we finally got off, I figured we'd be in Doggy Hawk. Instead, we were in a place called Elizabeth City, North Carolina. I heard Wilbur say that we are about 600 miles from home!

It turns out that we have to make another trip to get to Doggy Hawk. This time we will travel over water in something called a boat.

Wilbur found a room in a hotel. It's a place where travelers stay. I am learning so many new things.

Wilbur is out looking for a boat to take us to Doggy Hawk. I hope we will get going soon. It is so hot here, my tongue is hanging out. I heard someone say it is almost 100 degrees!

As soon as Wilbur left the room, Nibbles

stuck his head out of Wilbur's bag. I was so surprised to see him that I jumped. Thank goodness he was all right. The mouse had quite a tale.

He had tossed his cookies on the train, all right — in some lady's purse. Then he had crawled into Wilbur's bag, where he'd been hiding for days.

I knew Nibbles didn't want to fly. So I asked him why he'd come on the trip to Doggy Hawk.

"I don't want to play cat and mouse with Chester anymore," he said. "He's always trying to scare me. Sometimes I even think he wants to eat me."

"He's only playing," I told Nibbles. "Chester likes you."

"Cats like the way mice taste," said Nibbles. "Anyway, there is another reason I came on the trip. I'm hoping that you can make your dream come true and so can I. Maybe someone in Doggy Hawk will want me for a pet."

I want Nibbles's dream to come true. But I have never heard of a pet mouse.

September 11, 1900

We're sailing for Doggy Hawk!

Most people in Elizabeth City have never heard of the place. It took Wilbur a couple of days to find a boat to take us there. If you can call this broken-down tub a boat.

The sails are torn, the ropes are rotten, and it leaks. The cabin is dirty, too. It even smells bad. A dog would never choose to live like this.

Later

My adventure has turned into a nightmare! We are in the middle of a storm.

Thwack! Big waves crash onto the boat. Wind rips the sails.

Wilbur helps the crew bail water. He must be very brave, because he doesn't look scared at all.

Nibbles and I are scared, though. We went slipping and sliding across the deck. We were afraid we would be tossed overboard!

I wanted to fly in the air, not into the water.

So I grabbed Nibbles and ran into the cabin. Now we are huddled in a corner.

Nibbles does not look too good. I have never seen a mouse turn green before.

Being the world's first flying dog isn't easy. And I'm not even in the air yet.

September 12, 1900

Tonight we landed at Doggy Hawk. I don't see any dogs yet. Maybe that is because it is dark, and they are all asleep.

We are spending the night on the boat. I think Wilbur is tired and hungry. The cabin is so filthy and full of bugs, he has hardly eaten a thing since yesterday.

Nibbles and I like a clean kitchen, too. But we got so hungry we forgot about it for a while. Nibbles even found some cheese.

"I think I've bitten off more than I can chew," he said. I told him not to eat so fast.

"I'm not talking about the cheese," he said. "I'm talking about the trip." He still looked a little green. And he looked tired. Nibbles curled into a ball and wrapped his long tail around himself.

"Do you think there are pet mice in Doggy Hawk?" he asked me.

I didn't want to tell him what I thought. But by then Nibbles was already sleeping, so I didn't have to answer.

September 13, 1900

This morning we started out for William Tate's home. Along the way, I looked for dogs. I didn't see any. All I saw was sand and a couple of houses. There is a lifesaving station, too. That is where the men work who rescue people from boating accidents.

William Tate was very friendly. He shook Wilbur's hand and said, "Call me Bill." He patted me on the head.

Bill and his family fixed us ham and eggs. I love ham, but I'm not crazy about eggs. Bill sure was interested in flying. He wanted to hear all about the glider.

We're going to stay with the Tates for a

while. Their house isn't fancy, but at least I know where we'll sleep and where we'll eat. I'm starting to enjoy myself.

While Wilbur gets the glider ready, I can sniff around. I want to find the dogs that run things here. They could stand to fix the place up a little.

"This place doesn't look like the house in Dayton," Nibbles said when everyone had gone to bed. During the day, he had to stay hidden. "There isn't much furniture. They don't have any pictures. They don't have any books."

It's true. I think the reason they don't have much stuff is so they'll have less to dust. There is so much sand here, they'd be dusting forever.

September 14, 1900

It's a dog day. That means it's so hot my tongue hangs out all the time. I wish I could take off my coat.

Wilbur is putting the pieces of the glider together. Even in this heat, he keeps his shirt on.

He keeps his starched collar on. He even keeps his tie on.

That's the way men dress in Dayton. Not in Doggy Hawk. People stop and stare. You'd think he was wearing a costume.

Nobody wears starched collars here. They don't wear ties. Wilbur won't have to worry about pressing his pants.

Besides sand, there is a lot of something else at Doggy Hawk: little bugs called mosquitoes. They like to bite people the way fleas like to bite dogs. I think the mosquitoes bite Wilbur through his clothes. I'll bet they even bite through his socks. He is always scratching.

September 20, 1900

It's another dog day. Wilbur is still working on the glider. Mrs. Tate let him use her sewing machine to finish stitching fabric for the wings.

I met a dog from the lifesaving station. His name is Salty. I asked Salty where to find the dogs that ran Doggy Hawk.

"Woof," he said. That could mean a lot of

things. *Is he laughing at me?* I wondered. Then he asked if I was housebroken.

"Of course!" I answered. "What does that have to do with anything?"

"If you're old enough to be housebroken, you should know better," he yelped. "Doggy Hawk is just a name. This place isn't really run by dogs. It's run by people. Wise up, pup."

"I'm not a puppy!" I yelped as he trotted away. My tail drooped.

"I knew it was too good to be true," I told Nibbles.

"Cheer up," Nibbles told me. "You can still be happy about the name. This place isn't called Mousie Hawk, you know."

September 24, 1900

While he works, Wilbur talks to me about the glider. He must miss Orville, who usually does all the talking. I miss him, too.

But I learned a lot by listening to Wilbur. I found out why the curve of the wings will help the glider fly. It's not just for balance.

It takes the wind longer to go over the top of the curve than under it. That means the air on top has to move faster than the air underneath.

Now here is a startling fact: Slow-moving air can push harder than fast air. So the slow-moving air *under* the wing will push it *up.*

I bet I'm the only dog in the world who knows that. It makes my tail wag.

September 28, 1900

Orville is here! Now there is one other person in Doggy Hawk who dresses like Wilbur.

Orville was glad to see me. He and Katharine were afraid I had gotten lost somewhere. He kept petting me on the head and feeding me crackers.

Wilbur introduced Orville to the Tates. Then Orville met the guys from the lifesaving station.

What happened nearly knocked me off my paws. I thought Orville would start blabbing away. Instead, he shut up like a clam. I wondered why he was so quiet. I was afraid he was sick.

Later, when the Wright brothers were alone, Orville had plenty to say. I guess he's shy with people he doesn't know. But he's no scaredy-cat. I once met a scaredy-cat dalmatian. He was afraid of his own spots.

CHAPTER 6
October 1900

October 1, 1900

Wilbur and Orville are done putting the glider together. It measures 17 feet 5 inches from wingtip to wingtip and weighs about 50 pounds.

Nibbles took one look at it and whistled. "How are they going to get it off the ground?"

"With the wind," I told him. "Just like a kite."

There is a flap in front called an elevator. When it is tilted up or down, it makes the glider go up or down. The elevator makes the glider look like a big duck. Without the feathers, of course.

The glider has two sets of wings, just like

the little kite Orville and Wilbur built. The pilot (that's the person who flies the plane) has to lie down in the center of the lower wing. He'll move the elevator up and down with his hands.

The pilot will work the wing-warping by pushing his feet against a T-bar. The T-bar is connected to the wings with wires and pulleys. By pushing with his right or left foot, the pilot can twist the ends of the wings. When one wing twists up, the other twists down. I was glad the Wright brothers figured this out on their own. I'm not sure I would have thought of it.

I'm glad the glider isn't just a little kite anymore. But the size has me worried, too. The Wright brothers are both taller than I am. I can't reach the T-bar and the elevator at the same time the way they can. I want to be a pilot. How will I fly the glider?

Maybe I can jump back and forth. I'll push against the T-bar with my back paws. Then I'll leap forward and push the elevator with my front paws. I'll have to make some fast moves. But I'm ready to go!

October 2, 1900

I was all ready to fly today. But we never got the glider off the ground. Wilbur said there wasn't enough wind.

Wilbur and Orville stood around for hours watching the birds. Then they started running and flapping their arms like wings.

Uh-oh, I thought to myself. *Those guys have had too much sun.*

Then suddenly, it hit me. They were getting the feel of flying. They were learning more about how birds tilt their wings to balance in the air.

Salty brought some guys from the lifesaving station to watch. He looked at the Wright brothers and twirled his paw by his ear. "Cuckoo." He laughed.

I'll have the last laugh. The question is: When?

1900

ot the glider off the ground today!

s morning, Bill Tate loaded it into a wagon. Then we all went out to a place called Kill Devil Hills. It's a part of Doggy Hawk that looks like the Sahara Desert.

Bill helped Orville and Wilbur carry the glider up a big hill. Then Wilbur got inside the cutout in the center of the glider's lower wing. Bill and Orville grabbed the wingtips and all three of them ran into the wind.

Soon Wilbur jumped and pulled himself onto the lower wing. Bill and Orville grabbed the wingtips and ran into the wind. Wilbur put his feet against the T-bar. The wind flowed over the wings. Then the glider began to rise into the air!

"Let go!" shouted Wilbur. Bill and Orville stepped back. Wilbur went up, up, and away.

For a few moments, I held my breath, watching him glide on the wind. But before I could blink, the glider started to bob and shake.

"Get me down!" shouted Wilbur.

Orville and Bill pulled on the ropes attached to the sides of the glider. They brought it back down onto the sand.

It was all over. I was so upset I howled. The flight was over before it had really begun!

But Wilbur was just being careful. "I promised Katharine I'd take care of myself," he said.

I thought Wilbur had read my mind. Then I realized he was talking to Orville.

That night

I'm so excited I can hardly sleep. Tomorrow it will be my turn to fly the glider. I just know it. And I won't come down as quickly as Wilbur did.

October 4, 1900

It was a busy day. We moved out of the Tate house and set up camp at Kill Devil Hills. That way we can live right where we fly.

At first I was glad. Then Nibbles gave me some bad news. He told me he couldn't stay in the camp.

"I'm used to living indoors. I can't live outside in the sand. It's itchy, and there is no place to hide," he said. "I've decided to move to the lifesaving station. It's cozy there. The guys don't chase me, and there are plenty of crumbs."

He promised to come and visit.

Tonight Orville did the cooking over our campfire, and Wilbur washed the dishes. Then we all watched the sunset.

The sky lit up with beautiful blues and golds. I sat and thought about Nibbles up at the lifesaving station. I hoped he had some cheese.

I didn't get to fly today, but neither did the Wright brothers. There wasn't enough wind.

October 5, 1900

Bill said there was a whole house buried in the sand right where we pitched our tent. You can still see the top branches of a tree that was in the front yard.

Wind blew all that sand a long time ago. But there wasn't enough wind for anyone to fly today. Again.

October 6, 1900

Still not enough wind.

October 7, 1900

Still not.

October 8, 1900

Not.

October 9, 1900

There *still* isn't enough wind to send the glider into the air with a pilot. Instead, the Wright brothers have been flying it like a kite.

What good is having a flying machine if you can't fly in it?

October 10, 1900

Today we had a flying accident without even flying. The glider was on the ground when — *whoosh!* A gust of wind hit it.

It happened in a flash. The wind picked the

glider up and threw it 20 feet. When it landed, the whole right side was smashed.

My heart sank right down into my paws. I figured my chance to fly was over.

I was glad Nibbles wasn't around. It would have broken his heart to see a grown dog cry.

October 14, 1900

It took three days to fix the glider. Wouldn't you know it? There was plenty of wind the whole time.

Boom! Boom! Boom! At night the wind shook our tent and sounded like thunder. I couldn't get any sleep.

Lots of times we had to crawl outside and hold the tent down to keep it from blowing away. I always got sand in my eyes.

When there isn't enough wind, we can't fly. When there is too much, it wrecks everything.

I know I'm acting like a puppy, but I'm mad.

October 17, 1900

"Today we'll fly the glider with a pilot," Wilbur said to Orville. "But there isn't enough wind to lift either of us into the air. We need somebody who doesn't weigh so much."

I figured he meant me. Who else besides the Wright brothers knew all about the flying machine?

I got so excited, my fur stood on end. But when I ran toward the glider, Orville pulled me back.

They sent Bill Tate's nephew Tom into the air. They let a boy fly instead of me! I couldn't do a thing but stand there and chase my tail.

Fifi's words came back to haunt me. She said the Wright brothers would never let a dog into their flying machine. Maybe I've been barking up the wrong tree all this time. Maybe I won't ever fly after all.

October 18, 1900

Nibbles came down from the lifesaving station for a visit. He could tell my tail was dragging, so he tried to cheer me up.

"The glider isn't a real flying machine, anyway," he said. "It's just a big kite. You practically said so yourself. You didn't miss out on so much after all."

I thanked Nibbles for trying to make me feel better. Then I watched the birds flying around the tent. They didn't need wind to get off the ground. They flew when they wanted. They flew where they wanted.

Now *that* was flying.

October 23, 1900

We are leaving Doggy Hawk. I guess Wilbur and Orville have given up on flying. The glider is lying in the sand. Mrs. Tate's going to make dresses from the cloth that covers the wings.

I'm glad we're leaving. I'm sick of sand. I'm

sick of wind. I'm sick of not flying. I guess you could say I'm sick as a dog.

Just when I thought things couldn't get any worse, they did. Nibbles told me he was saying good-bye.

"I can't face another journey," he said. His whiskers twitched. "Tell Fifi and Chester I'll miss them."

I tried to talk Nibbles into coming home. But he wouldn't change his mind.

"My home is here. The guys at the lifesaving station feed me now. They all like me. I don't have to hide. I have become a pet mouse."

I'm glad that Nibbles's dream has come true. But what about mine?

October 30, 1900

When I got home, I had lots of explaining to do. I had to tell Chester and Fifi where I had been. I also had to tell them that Nibbles wasn't coming back.

They were both sad, but Chester took it the hardest. For days, he sat by Nibbles's mouse hole without moving. Fifi said he was "catatonic." That's a fancy word for staying still.

"I shouldn't have teased him so much," Chester kept howling. "It's all my fault that he's gone."

I guess Chester really loved that mouse. His tough-cat routine was just an act.

"Kitty, don't cry over spilled milk," Fifi told him. "Let's be happy for Nibbles. His dream has come true. He's a pet mouse now." Then she asked me about the flying machine.

I told her it was bogus. A fake. Nothing but a kite.

Fifi stared at me. "Aha!" she said. "They didn't let you fly." Then she told me it didn't matter because happiness was right under my own backyard.

Maybe she's right. I'm going out to the backyard, and I'm going to dig a hole. Then I'm going to bury this diary in it. And I'm going to forget all about flying forever.

Chapter 7
September 1903

September 10, 1903

Holding this diary makes me feel like a young dog again. Time flies, even if I didn't. There's a lot to catch up on.

For one thing, I'm a dad. Last year I fell in love with a dog named Foxy. We've got puppies of our own. There's a girl, Ruby, and two boys, Sam and Sparky.

Foxy is a Border terrier — just like me! I met her when she moved in next door. She was three years old.

Foxy and I hit it off right away. She is the spunkiest dog I know. Right after she moved in, she caught Chester strutting through her yard. "Yap! Yap! Yap! Get out!" she told him. She raised such a ruckus that Chester beat it.

Chester never went into Foxy's yard again. He never teases her, either. I think she scared him, and Chester doesn't scare easily.

While I was busy with my new family, the Wright brothers were busy with other things. Wilbur and Orville went back to Doggy Hawk two more times, in 1901 and 1902. Each time, they took a bigger glider. They kept changing things to try to make it fly better. They wanted it to stay in the air longer.

From what I heard, sometimes things got better. Sometimes things got worse. They always said they learned from their mistakes.

I never tried to go with them again. I still didn't think a glider was a real flying machine. It couldn't fly with its own power, like a bird.

I'd made up my mind to forget about flying. But I never *really* forgot.

Last winter I was sitting on the porch with Chester and Fifi. A horseless carriage went by.

I had heard of them, but this was the only one I had ever seen. It was powered by a motor.

The bicycle wheels in my head started spinning. If a motor could power a buggy, a motor could power a glider. Then the glider wouldn't have to depend on the wind.

I had to tell Orville and Wilbur somehow. I decided the time had come to take a chance. I had to write them a note. There was no other way.

I didn't dare tell Fifi and Chester what I was going to do. That night, after Wilbur had gone to sleep, I barked and woke him up. I showed him the message I had written.

Put a motor on it.

Then I woke Orville. I showed him the note, too.

The next morning I waited to see what would happen. Would they remember what I had done?

Wilbur and Orville looked at each other across the breakfast table. "I had the strangest dream last night," they both said at the same time. Pretty soon they were talking about powering a glider with a motor.

Whew! The Wright brothers thought they had dreamed up the idea themselves. It was just what I'd been hoping for.

A few days later, the bickering started all over again. This time it made me happy. It meant they were figuring out the best way to build the new flying machine.

The other day I told the pups a little about the Wright brothers and their glider. Then I told them what my mom and dad told me: A terrier never gives up.

Then I went out and dug up this diary. It's old and dog-eared, but that doesn't matter.

"It's time to show the pups what it means to be a terrier," Foxy told me. "Go back to Doggy Hawk and finish the book about a dog's first flight."

September 14, 1903

Today I got Fifi and Chester together and told them my plan. I was going back to Doggy Hawk.

It was just like old times. Chester said, "Kitty Hawk."

I said, "Doggy."

We were at it again. *Kitty. Doggy. Kitty. Doggy.*

Until Fifi howled at us to stop.

She gave me the old line about happiness being under my backyard. But deep down she knew that a terrier's gotta do what a terrier's gotta do.

September 15, 1903

The pups wanted to know more about the flying machine.

I told them all about it. The whole story of the model and making the drawings. All about balance and wind. The whole nine yards.

By the time I finished, I was panting. But the kids barked for more.

So I told them how the Wright brothers built their own motor this year. They built two propellers, too. Those are long blades that will whirl around on the front of the plane.

Sparky, my scrappy son, had to know why the airplane needed propellers. Here is what I told him:

The motor turns the propellers. The propellers pull the plane forward. As the plane moves forward, the wings move through the air, which pushes the wings up. Now that the flying machine has a motor and propellers, it will fly like a bird. It won't have to depend on the wind.

By the time I had explained all of that, the other puppies were asleep. But Sparky was still wide awake. So I told him how the flying machine was my idea. I told him about going back to Doggy Hawk.

"Dad," he said, "I hope you fly this time. Someday I want to be a pilot, too."

I won't let Sparky down.

September 17, 1903

I took the family down to the bike shop to see how the flying machine was coming along. It was all in pieces. "Bow-WOW! It's going to be big," Foxy said.

PROPELLER

The bike shop is almost completely filled with parts. There is hardly any room left for Wilbur and Orville, let alone any customers.

This won't be just a glider. It will be a *real* flying machine. The Wright brothers have started calling it an airplane.

"Are you really going to fly that thing, Dad?" my pups asked me again and again.

I always gave the same answer.

"Yip."

September 19, 1903

Today I heard some news that made my tail wag. The Wright brothers are taking me with them to Doggy Hawk! I don't have to sneak along this time. I've been hanging around the airplane so much they have given me a nick-name: Flyer.

This time I won't wait for them to let me fly. I'll take matters into my own paws. When I see my chance, I'll grab it.

September 20, 1903

We'll be leaving any day now.

I promised Foxy I would be extra careful. She wants to make sure I don't get caught writing in this diary. Chester and Fifi have been telling her scary stories about the three-ring circus. So I'll put down only the very most important stuff. I don't want the family to wind up in the side show!

September 22, 1903

Tomorrow we leave for Doggy Hawk.

This time I said good-bye to everyone. Fifi gave me an extra warning to keep the diary out of sight.

September 26, 1903

Here I am at Doggy Hawk again. I forgot there was so much sand.

Guess who was waiting on the dock at Doggy Hawk bay? My old friend Nibbles. Was I ever glad to see him!

He said he just had a feeling I'd show up. He said he knew because his tail had been itching for days.

Nibbles and I spent some time catching up. I told him about Foxy and the pups. He said he'd met a nice lady mouse. Her name was Sandy.

I am glad to see Nibbles so happy. Now I have to make my own dream come true.

Chapter 8
October 1903

October 5, 1903

Winter arrived in Doggy Hawk early this year. On my last visit, it was sweltering hot. Now it keeps getting colder.

The Wright brothers have started building a big storage room for the airplane. It's called a hangar. That is where they will put the plane together.

While they were busy, I took a little stroll and ran into Salty, my old pal from the lifesaving station. He gave me an earful.

"If anyone can fly, it's the Wright brothers," he said. He sure had changed his tune.

He said last year's glider really took off. The guys had put a tail on it. The tail helped to steer the plane. He said they called the tail a rudder.

I told Salty that he hadn't seen anything yet. This year we had a *real* flying machine.

October 10, 1903

Wilbur and Orville have been putting the pieces of the plane together. I'm leaving the work to them. I want to spend lots of time with Nibbles. Every day, I visit him at the lifesaving station.

The first time I went, I couldn't believe my eyes. Nibbles and Sandy sit right out in the open. Nobody chases them away. The guys in the crew even play with them. One of them, Jeff Daniels, feeds them crumbs. I've never seen Nibbles so happy.

October 16, 1903

Things are not going well. The weather has been terrible. We have had storm after storm. Rain pours from the sky. The wind howls. Sometimes it blows so hard that it knocks down part of the hangar walls. Once it tore off the shed door. Almost every time it storms, Wilbur and Orville have to repair one of the buildings.

The storms scare me so much! I am glad Nibbles is safe inside the lifesaving station.

October 21, 1903

The temperature keeps dropping. I know that Wilbur and Orville are cold. My coat keeps me warm and comfortable.

Even though it is cold, the Wright brothers keep working away. The end is not in sight. We have had more storms.

October 28, 1903

I've been trying to be so careful, I haven't written much at all! But last night I had a close call. Orville caught me writing in the diary. He looked right at me.

I had to think fast. I sat on the diary and nosed the pen under my blanket.

Luckily for me, Orville just couldn't believe his eyes. I guess he thought he was dreaming.

It feels like winter is here, even though it's only October. Every morning, the water in my dish is frozen. We have had snow already, and the wind is freezing cold.

The Wright brothers made a stove out of a can. It was nice and warm but it made so much smoke, my eyes watered. So did Wilbur's and Orville's. They looked like they were crying. For days everything was covered with soot.

Then Orville made a pipe for the stove. The smoke went up through the pipe instead of all over the place. The stove worked fine.

I'm going to have to be extra *extra* careful about writing. I don't want another close call.

Chapter 9
November 1903

November 5, 1903

The airplane is finally finished. It is the biggest flying machine the Wright brothers have ever built. It weighs 750 pounds, and the wingspan is 40½ feet! It is different from the old flying machines in other ways, too. It has a motor and propellers. And there is a lever to operate the front elevator. There is also what the Wright brothers call a hip cradle. Wilbur and Orville can control the wing-warping and rudder with it. The pilot just has to lean his hips left or right.

I think the new controls will make it easier for me to fly the plane. I can grab the lever with my teeth. I can move the hip cradle with my feet. If I get the chance to fly, that is. I have to believe that I will.

November 7, 1903

What a letdown! Yesterday the Wright brothers took the plane out of the hangar. Then they started up the motor.

That motor let out a roar. The propellers started to turn. The plane rattled. The wings bounced and the tail shook. The front elevator that looks like a duckbill flapped like mad. Then parts started to come off the plane.

Wilbur turned the motor off. He said some important pieces got broken. I thought we were ready to fly. Now I'll have to wait some more.

November 11, 1903

The Wright brothers have sent for some new parts. I hope these will be stronger. Meanwhile, it keeps getting colder. Even my coat doesn't help me stay warm anymore.

The stove doesn't keep us warm enough, either. At night we pile on the blankets and quilts. We are up to five blankets and two quilts each.

November 17, 1903

Now we are up to five blankets, two quilts, and a hot-water jug each. Next I think the Wright brothers will sleep with all their clothes on. What can I do? I'm already wearing mine.

November 18, 1903

Wilbur and Orville have made a track for the airplane. The plane will roll down the track until it builds enough speed to take off into the air.

The way they made the track is smart. It is in four 15-foot sections. The plane can roll for 60 feet. If that isn't long enough, the back section can be picked up and moved to the front. The plane can roll for 15 more feet. If that still isn't enough, they move the back section forward again.

I just wish we could get rolling.

November 20, 1903

The new parts are here! I should be up in the air any day now.

November 21, 1903

Should be any day now.

November 22, 1903

Any day now.

November 23, 1903

Any day . . .

November 24, 1903

The new parts aren't strong enough. The motor still makes the airplane shake. It shakes some more when the propellers whirl. The shaking makes the parts rattle and roll. Then they fall off and break.

Getting off the ground is a lot harder than I thought. When I came up with the idea of flying, I didn't think it would be this tough. Birds make it look so easy.

I'm cold. I miss Foxy. I miss the puppies. I want to go home.

But I can't give up. I want to fly. I have to finish my book about a dog's first flight. I can't let Foxy and the pups down.

Chapter 10
December 1903

December 2, 1903

Orville has left to go back home to Dayton. He will make some new parts himself.

I almost had to tie myself up to keep from following him. I tried and tried to think of how to get a message back home. All I could do was leave some paw prints on his coat.

December 8, 1903

We are now up to six blankets, four quilts, and a hot-water jug each. How long can this go on? This cold makes my teeth chatter so much I can hardly write.

December 11, 1903

Orville is back with the new parts he made himself. I am keeping my paws crossed.

December 12, 1903

The Wright brothers put the new parts on the plane. Then they started the motor. I held my breath.

The motor roared. The plane began to rattle and shake. The front elevator flapped up and down. The whole airplane started to bounce.

I shut my eyes. After a moment I heard Orville laughing. Then I heard Wilbur's voice. "Success!"

When I opened my eyes, the Wright brothers were grinning. They slapped each other on the back. Now we are going to fly!

December 15, 1903

We still haven't gotten off the ground. Instead, the Wright brothers find something else to do every day. They keep tinkering with the plane. Then they talk about the best place to build the starting track. It's always something. Let's get in the air!

December 16, 1903

Nibbles thinks tomorrow is the big day. He says his tail has been itching. I don't see how he can feel a thing. His tail looks like an icicle and Nibbles looks like a mousecicle. It's so cold I can't even wag my own tail.

The winter is getting worse and worse. If we don't fly soon, I'm afraid it will be too late. The weather might be too rough for flying.

Wilbur knew I was worried. "Cheer up, Flyer," he said. I want to make my nickname come true.

December 17, 1903

The minute I woke up, I said to myself, *Today is the day.* I could feel it in my frozen bones. My dream was going to come true. I just had to wait for my chance.

The Wright brothers brought the airplane

out of the hangar. Then they hoisted a signal flag.

Nibbles was on the lookout at the lifesaving station. He showed up by the time the track was laid down. He brought the crew from the station with him, and Sandy, too. Even Salty was there.

The Wright brothers tossed a coin to see who would fly. Orville won.

He set up his big box camera. Then he showed Jeff Daniels from the lifesaving station how to use it. Orville told him to take a picture when the plane took off.

Then Orville and Wilbur walked a little ways away. They talked to each other for a few moments. Then they shook hands.

Orville got into the pilot's position. He was wearing his suit and tie.

The motor coughed and sputtered. Then it began to roar. The propellers turned. The plane shuddered and shook, but it didn't come apart. Nothing broke.

When it started down the track, everyone clapped and cheered.

It was now or never. All eyes were on the airplane. I ran forward and leaped onto Orville's back.

Just as the plane began to take off, I felt a gust of wind. It blew sand into the air. Orville got some in his eyes. He couldn't see well enough to fly the plane!

The flap called the elevator started to dip. The nose of the plane was going down! I grabbed the control lever with my teeth and pulled it up. I pushed Orville's body to the right, against the hip cradle.

I was flying the plane! At last, I could feel the wind beneath my paws.

My career as a pilot only lasted a moment, until Orville blinked the sand out of his eyes. But I know I'll never forget it.

Then suddenly, I was thrown into the air. I hit the sand hard and tumbled over and over. *Ow!* I hit my head.

I didn't let it slow me down. I ran over to the front of the crowd.

Everyone was cheering and clapping and jumping up and down. Then the strangest thing happened. They all got real quiet.

Some people started shaking their heads. Others just stared at the plane with their mouths hanging open. It was like they had just seen a miracle.

I couldn't help myself. Suddenly, I blurted out, "I flew the plane! I flew the plane!"

I didn't think those people would understand me. I figured all they'd hear was *woof, ruff-ruff,* and *yip.*

But they were all staring at me.

The plane touched down and Orville ran to me. "It's true!" he said. "The dog flew the plane."

A hush fell over the crowd. Then suddenly, someone shouted, "Put that dog in a three-ring circus!"

Soon everyone was shouting, "Put that dog in the circus! Put that dog in the circus! Put that dog in the circus!" Then everything went black.

Later

The next thing I knew, I was lying in the shed next to the stove. I opened my eyes and looked up at Nibbles. "What happened?" I yelped.

"You flew," Nibbles whispered. "But you fell off the plane and hit your head."

Then he told me everyone thought Orville was the only one in the plane. Even Orville didn't know what really happened. By the time he got the sand out of his eyes, I was on the ground.

"What about the picture?" I asked.

I was one lucky dog. Jeff Daniels snapped the picture of Orville flying the plane a second before I jumped aboard. I would stay out of the circus and go home to my family.

I jumped up and barked for joy. I must have blacked out after my fall. Nobody wanted to put me in the circus after all. It was all a bad dream!

Except for the part about flying. That was a dream come true.

December 18, 1903

That airplane flight only lasted 12 seconds. But for the first time in history, a flying machine had flown with its own power. It had carried Orville and me into the air like a bird.

The Wright brothers named that plane after me. *Flyer.*

Wilbur and Orville took turns and made three more flights. The longest one was at noon that same day. Wilbur flew a distance of 852 feet for 59 seconds!

But before they could try again, a gust of wind tumbled the *Flyer* over and over in the sand. It was completely wrecked.

After that, the Wright brothers headed down to the telegraph office. They sent a telegram back to Dayton, telling Katharine and all the folks back home the good news. I knew Foxy and the pups would find out, too. I wished I could see their faces.

December 19, 1903

We were all packed and ready to leave Doggy Hawk. I went to the lifesaving station to say good-bye to Nibbles and Sandy.

Nibbles and I knew we would never see each other again. I wanted the last thing I said to him to be special. What could I say? My feelings seemed too big for words.

I had to think very hard. Then I knew what to tell him.

"Nibbles, you'll always be my best friend."

"You'll always be mine, too, Angus," he said. "Say hello to Chester and Fifi for me."

The Wright brothers were calling me. It was time to leave.

"Take care of him, Sandy," I said.

As I turned to go, Nibbles waved good-bye. Now both our dreams had come true.

December 25, 1903

Being home is the best Christmas present I could have. Foxy and the puppies were thrilled about my flight. As for Fifi and Chester, they took the news a little differently.

"I don't believe it," Fifi snapped.

"It never happened," Chester meowed.

I couldn't blame them. That is what almost everyone said.

My mom always said, "Seeing is believing." I guess that's true. I think one day everybody will see airplanes flying up in the sky. Planes will fly for hours and hours.

Only a few newspapers carried the story of the first airplane flight. The ones that did got it all wrong. They even said thc first flight happened in a place called KITTY HAWK. The wrong namc will go down in history.

I don't know how it happened. Chester won't admit anything, but I bet that cat had something to do with it.

I know what I know. I saw what I saw. AND IT WAS DOGGY HAWK.

Well, my dream has come true, and my diary is finished. When the world is ready to know how smart dogs really are, they can read it.

Then they'll know how a dog helped get the Wright brothers off the ground. Until that day, this will remain hidden. I have learned of other diaries written by dogs. They tell about history as we saw it. This is my story.

P.S. Foxy says this will be an important history book, so I have to tell the truth. I hate to admit it, but Chester was right. The first airplane flight was at Kitty Hawk. I only pretended the name was Doggy Hawk. But that is what I will always think it should have been called.

Stuff I've Learned About Flying

When I was a puppy, I thought I knew everything. But I had a lot to learn. Over the years, I've found out lots of useful stuff.

Some of what I learned came from listening to Wilbur and Orville. Other stuff came from listening to Katharine. She was a schoolteacher.

I learned some more from books. Otis Smoot, the guard at the library, took a liking to me after a while. He let me hang around and read.

Before Wilbur and Orville, people had been trying to fly for thousands of years. Some of them tied feathers to their arms and flapped them like wings. I could have told them it wouldn't work.

In an ancient Greek legend, a man named Icarus flew with wings made of wax. The sun melted his wings, and he drowned in the ocean. I'm glad that it is just a made-up story.

Around 1500, Leonardo da Vinci made

drawings of flying machines. But they never got off the ground.

In 1783, in France, the Montgolfier brothers sent a sheep, a duck, and a rooster into the sky. They used a hot-air balloon. There was a problem, though. A hot-air balloon wasn't easy to steer.

I was surprised to learn that other people had made gliders before the Wright brothers. But Wilbur and Orville were the first to make a glider with a wing-warping control. They thought that once they could balance the glider, putting the motor on it would be easy. It wasn't so easy after all, but it worked.

Like I said, they thought the motor was their idea. But I know the truth. Now you do, too.

Stuff I've Learned About Terriers

Dogs like me are called terriers. The name *terrier* comes from *terra,* the Latin word for "earth." Terriers were bred to burrow in the earth and drive out small animals, like mice.

I was shocked when I read that. I would never go after Nibbles!

Terriers are known for being spunky and full of energy. There are 25 kinds of terrier breeds. Foxy and I are Border terriers.